Jack and the Beanstalk

The Princess and the Pea

Elizabeth Laird
illustrated by Simone Lia

First published in Great Britain 2000
by Mammoth
an imprint of Egmont Children's Books Limited
239 Kensington High Street, London W8 6SA
10 9 8 7 6 5 4 3 2 1

Text by Elizabeth Laird ©
Egmont Children's Books Limited 2000
Illustrations copyright © Simone Lia 2000

ISBN 0 7497 3818 9

A CIP catalogue record for this title is available from the British Library

Printed in Hong Kong

Jack and the Beanstalk

There was once a poor woman whose only son was a brave boy called Jack. They lived all alone with Milky-White, their cow, and often they did not have enough to eat.

One day, Jack's mother said to him, "There's no food left in the house at all. We'll have to sell Milky-White, poor thing. Jack, take her to market and get the best price you can."

So Jack walked off down the road, leading the cow to market. On the way, he met an old man.

"Is that cow for sale?" the old man asked.

"Yes," said Jack, "for the best price I can find."

"I'll give you five beans for her," the old man said, "and you'll never regret it, for they are the finest beans in the world."

Jack took the beans, and gave Milky-White to the old man, and he went back home to his mother.

"You were very quick," his mother said. "What price did you get for Milky-White?"

"Five beans," said Jack, "and we'll never regret it, for they are the finest beans in the world."

His mother was furious when she saw that Jack had sold their cow for a handful of beans. In her rage she threw them out of the window and sent Jack to bed without any supper.

Next morning, when Jack woke up, his room was dark. He ran to the window and looked out. A giant beanstalk was growing outside his window, up and up to the sky, so high that its head was lost in the clouds.

At once Jack ran outside and began to climb the beanstalk. He climbed and climbed, higher and higher, until at last he came to a country in the sky. A road stretched out in front of him and Jack began to walk along it.

Soon he came to an enormous castle. Slipping under the gate, he found himself right by the foot of a giant woman. She bent down low to look at him.

Jack felt scared but he said bravely, "Please can you give me something to eat?"

The giantess laughed. "You're a cheeky lad," she said. "Don't you know that my husband eats boys for breakfast? Never mind. You're a nice-looking boy, and I'll hide you if he comes."

So she took Jack into her kitchen and gave him a slice of bread as big as a door.

A few minutes later the ground trembled as the giant's huge feet approached the castle, and a deep voice roared,

"Fee-fi-fo-fum,

I smell the blood of an Englishman.

Be he alive or be he dead

I'll grind his bones to make my bread."

"Quick," said the giant's wife. "My husband's coming. Into the pot with you," and she scooped Jack up in her hand and hid him in a pot.

The giant came into the room and sat down. His legs were as round as tree trunks and his eyes were as big as saucers.

"Is there boy for breakfast today?" he said to his wife.

"No," she answered, "just bacon," and she piled a mountain of bacon onto his plate and went off to hang out the washing.

When he had finished his breakfast, the giant took out some bags of gold and began to count them, but soon his head nodded and his eyes closed and snores as loud as thunder filled the air. He had fallen asleep.

As quick as a wink, Jack scrambled out of the pot, and heaving a bag of gold onto his shoulder, he made off as fast as he could, running out of the castle and down the road and scrambling down the beanstalk.

His mother was very pleased to see him, and for a long time they lived well on the giant's gold.

One day, when the gold was all spent, Jack set off up the beanstalk again. Just as before, he came to the giant's castle, and just as before the giant's wife kindly hid him.

Then the ground began to shake as the giant's huge feet tramped up to the castle, and an echoing voice bellowed,

"Fee-fi-fo-fum,

I smell the blood of an Englishman.

Be he alive or be he dead

I'll grind his bones to make my bread."

"Quick," said the giant's wife. My husband's coming. Into the basket with you," and she scooped Jack up in her hand and hid him in a basket.

The giant came into the room and sat down. His arms were as long as branches and his mouth was as big as a cave.

"Have you got boy for me today?" he said to his wife.

"No," she answered, "just sausages," and she piled a mass of sausages onto his plate.

When he had finished his breakfast, the giant fetched a hen from the coop, and when he said, "Lay!" the hen laid a golden egg.

"I must have that hen," thought Jack, and he waited until the giant's head began to nod, and his eyes began to close and snores as loud as thunder filled the air.

As quick as a wink, Jack scrambled out of the basket, and grabbing the hen, he made off as fast as he could, running out of the castle and down the road and scrambling down the beanstalk.

His mother was not at all pleased to see the hen.

"Why didn't you bring some more gold?" she said.

But Jack put the hen on the table and said, "Lay!"

At once the hen laid a golden egg, and Jack's mother kissed him with delight. From then on they lived like kings on the gold the hen provided for them.

But the day came when Jack felt in need of another adventure, and he climbed the beanstalk again. This time he didn't let the giant's wife know he was there. He was afraid she would realise he had stolen her husband's gold and his hen.

Soon the ground began to shake as the giant's huge feet came near the castle, and a loud grating voice growled,

> *"Fee-fi-fo-fum,*
> *I smell the blood of an Englishman.*
> *Be he alive or be he dead*
> *I'll grind his bones to make my bread."*

The giant came into the room and sat down. His neck was as strong as a pillar and his beard was as thick as a bush.

"I can smell boy," he said to his wife, "as clear as clear can be."

"Aha," said the giant's wife, "it must be that wicked one who stole your gold and your magic hen," and the two of them began to hunt for Jack. They searched high and low, in every nook and cranny, but Jack had hidden in a copper pan, and they never thought to look in there.

At last they gave up looking and the giant's wife gave the giant a plate piled high with eggs. When the giant had finished eating, he fetched a golden harp out of a cupboard.

"Play!" he said, and at once the harp started to play the most beautiful music Jack had ever heard.

"I must have that harp," thought Jack, and he waited until the giant's head began to nod, and his eyes began to close and snores as loud as thunder filled the air.

As quick as a wink, Jack scrambled out of the copper pan, and snatching up the heavy harp, he ran off as fast as he could, out of the castle and down the road.

But the harp cried out, "Master! Save me!"

At once the giant woke up. With a roar of fury he leaped to his feet and began to run after Jack, and his feet shook the ground for miles around.

In the nick of time, Jack came to the top of the beanstalk and began to scramble down. When he got to the bottom he shouted to his mother, "Quick, Mother! Bring an axe!"

Then Jack cut the beanstalk through with the axe, and it fell to the ground and the giant crashed down with it. He lay still and never opened his eyes again for he was quite dead.

Jack and his mother lived long and happy lives.
The harp played for them whenever they wanted it to,
and the hen never ceased to lay her golden eggs.

The Princess
and the Pea

Once upon a time there was a prince who wanted to marry a real princess. He travelled far and wide to find a girl to suit him, but none of them would do. Some were beautiful and some were clever, but there were no real princesses among them.

"If I don't find a real princess, I'll marry no one at all," the Prince declared to the King and Queen.

One night a terrible storm raged around the castle. Lightning sliced through the sky and thunder rolled round the treetops. The rain came down in torrents.

Suddenly a knocking was heard at the castle gates, and when the Prince opened it, he found a girl standing outside.

"Let me in!" she begged. "I'm a princess."

"A princess?" said the Prince doubtfully, for the girl was soaking wet and her shoes were full  of mud. Yet for all that, she looked beautiful and clever, and the Prince liked her very well.

"A princess, is she?" sniffed the Queen. "We'll soon see about that," and she went off to make a bed where the Princess could sleep for the night.

First the Queen sent to the kitchens for a pea, and laid it on the bedstead. Then she piled on top of it twenty mattresses and twenty eiderdowns.

"Sleep well, my dear," she said to the Princess, "for your bed is as soft as can be."

In the morning, when the Princess came down to breakfast, the Queen asked her how she had slept.

"Badly, very badly," said the poor Princess. "There was something so hard in my bed that I'm black and blue all over."

The King and Queen were delighted.

"You must be a real princess, to feel a pea under twenty mattresses and twenty eiderdowns!" they said.

The Prince was delighted too.

"Marry me at once," he said.

The Princess agreed, and they were married next day, and no one ever put a pea in the Princess's bed again.